Blue Marble Sandcastle, The Adventure Of A Restless Warrior, *is intended to speak to the* *"Restless Warrior" that lives within each of us as we wrestle in the arena of self-discovery. May this book inspire readers with the necessary courage and endurance to continue on the path of their hearts' journey.*

The Author

◆

" A marvelously told story ....Sophisticated .....Unique...."

Dr. Richard D'Ambrosio, Bestselling Author, NO LANGUAGE BUT A CRY, LEONORA, COMPULSION

Dedicated to You
In hope that the Adult remembers
and the Child doesn't forget

◆

Special Dedication to
Dad and Nonna

◆

Special Thanks to:
MOM, EDGARDO, ANNETTA, CINDY, AND RON

BLUE MARBLE SANDCASTLE

The Adventure Of A Restless Warrior

by
Barbara Centrella

PUBLICATIONS - SIRRI - RAVENNA - ITALY

Once upon a timeless day, in a not so far away land, there lived a restless Warrior. He was restless because he was searching. Searching constantly for unconditional love, true harmony, and ultimately, total bliss.

This search was a difficult one for the Warrior because he lived in an emotionally confused and deeply frightened world.

The people of this world wallowed in sorrow, speaking only of fears, listening for new torments and seeking only the bleak.

This was not because they were evil, but because it was all they knew, and it was much too frightening to be a soul searching Warrior. That was reserved for the special few who could muster enough courage to look within.

Those courageous few knew how to harness the magical powers everyone is given, but seldom use, and tap into the music of the universe to find this bliss - even if just for a moment.

This was no easy task! Especially in a world that at one
time had been ruled by the notorious King Egos, an evil king
who reigned a long time ago when humans were not fully
evolved.

There are different legends regarding how King Egos
disappeared.

The most popular legend states that King Egos vanished when his wild horse, Destiny, drove him off a cliff.

The impact from the fallen horse and the heavily armored King rose to the skies like an explosion. Nothing but dust was in the skies for three days.

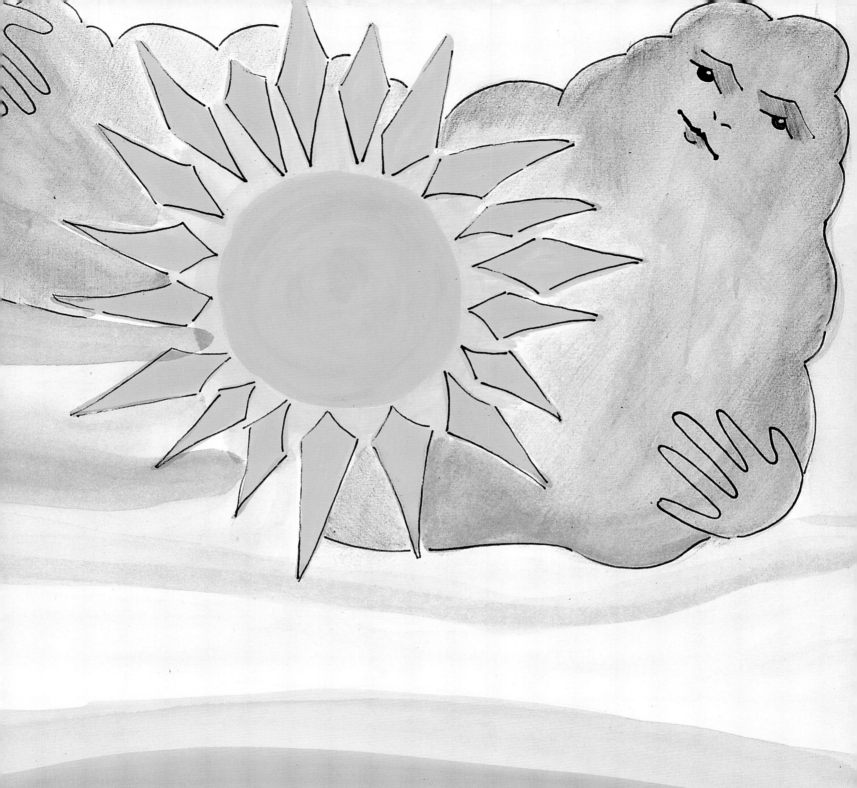

The dust was then named Shadow Of Doubt, and it was claimed that it would create doubt in the hearts and minds of those who permitted themselves to be weak and vulnerable. Rumor has it the shadow still lurks.

One day the Warrior was fidgety. He could not sit still. He had to move, do something, go somewhere. His heart screamed out to him.

"Your restlessness shall cease if you go for a walk along the beach. There you shall find a big surprise. For when you listen to me, a whole new world you shall see!"

The Little Warrior chose to obey his heart and set off on his journey.

He invited everyone he saw to join him on his little
adventure.

First he came upon Little Miss Busy.

"Little Miss Busy, would you like to come with me for a
walk along the magical strip by the sea?" asked the Little
Warrior eagerly.

"Of course not, Little Warrior!" replied Little Miss Busy.
"I'm much too busy - busy with nothing."
"Oh." sighed the Warrior, "Too bad."
And he moved on.

Suddenly he saw Bossy Buck.

"Oh, hello Mr. Bossy Buck!" exclaimed the Warrior.

"I'm going for a very special walk along the golden beaches. Would you care to come along?"

"No!" Bossy Buck replied.

"Can't you see I'm too busy telling people what they should be doing? Why are you going for a walk, anyway?" Bossy Buck asked.

"My heart told me to go." replied the bewildered Warrior.

"Don't you know," snorted Bossy Buck. "If every one followed their heart's journey no work would get done?"

The restless Warrior gazed up curiously and raised his eyebrows. Though his confidence was shaken by Bossy Buck's reply, he continued on his journey.

Shortly thereafter, the dejected Little Warrior met Madame Patience.

"Madame Patience, would you care to join me on my heart's journey along the beautiful beach?" asked the warrior hopefully.

"No thank you." responded Madame Patience. "I'm waiting."

"Waiting for what?" questioned the Warrior.

"Why I'm waiting for my life to take form" responded Madame Patience.

"Hmmmm." replied the Warrior, and he continued towards the shore.

The Warrior was feeling lonely and felt he should turn
around and just forget about his heart's journey to who knows
where, but something inside his heart forced him to march on
all alone.

The Warrior grew more and more curious with each step.
"Wow, where am I going?" he asked himself.
"Am I doing the right thing?" he continued.

Just before Shadow Of Doubt could creep up on him he heard his name being called.

"Little Warrior!" he heard from a distance. The Little Warrior stopped in his tracks and looked all around to see where the distant voice was coming from, but there appeared to be no one in sight.

"Little Warrior!" He heard again. Then he looked down in front of him and discovered a tiny person with a huge smile and a big beach ball staring back up at him.

"Hello, Little Warrior." said the tiny person. "I want to play. Will you play with me?"

"Yes! I would love to!" exclaimed the Warrior.

"I needed a rest from my journey and I wanted to stop and play. Isn't it strange that you asked me?" questioned the Warrior.

"No." replied the tiny person. "Not strange, but perfect!" And he threw the ball to the Warrior.

The Warrior caught the ball and asked,

"What is your name?"

"What do you wish my name to be?" responded the Warriors new playmate.

"Hmmmm." thought the Warrior. "I wish your name to be Dreamon, for I love the way that sounds."

"Then Dreamon shall be my name when I'm with you!"

"Wow, this is fun!" said the Warrior as he continued to play with his newly found friend.

"I'm delighted you stopped to play with me. You have really made me happy. Thank you!"

"It was my pleasure." responded the Warrior gratefully.

"Do you want to go someplace?" asked the tiny person.

"Yes I do." replied the Warrior. "Thank you for reminding me. You see I'm on a journey of some kind upon which my heart has sent me. I don't know exactly where it will lead, but I'm sure it will be quite an adventure! Would you like to come along?" the Warrior questioned his new friend.

"Oh, no thanks. It's too far and I don't know where you are going. It's your heart's journey, not mine. I must stay here. You are welcome to stay here with me and continue playing if you change your mind about your adventure." stated Dreamon.

"Oh how I would love to but I really must go." And the Warrior moved on.

The tiny person cried out his name in the distance. The Warrior felt a twinge of pain in his chest - as if he were leaving, forever, his little friend.

In spite of this, he firmly walked on, waving and smiling back at his small friend. The Little Warrior was never to see Dreamon again.

After he was through waving and smiling, the Warrior,
once again, found himself all alone, walking to nowhere.
A journey of which only his heart knew but would not tell.
But the Warrior was becoming eager to discover where this
little adventure would lead, so, he stayed on course.

By this time it was very dark. Not a soul was in sight, for no one was out at night. Most of the people could only see in the day. Usually the thieves and cheats came out at night because the darkness of the night made it easy to take advantage of the frightened people's lack of sight.

In spite of this our Little Warrior carried on, unafraid, protected by faith in his heart's journey.

The restless Warrior felt a certain love and confidence surround him. He became very relaxed and realized that his restlessness had ceased quite some time ago, but that he had just become aware of that fact now.

Suddenly he was overcome by a tremendous feeling of joy. Within seconds he became invisible and stepped into another realm; a new dimension where all dreams would come true.

The Warrior then recognized that the world was in the palm of his hand and that he was an essential part of the universe, and that the universe was an essential part of him.

The Warrior felt tingly all over, and his heart raced. But deep within the vigorous beating of his heart a dazzling sense of tranquility poured forth. A stillness so profound that the Warrior decided to stop in his tracks and take a deep breath.

All at once he came upon a gigantic castle of sand.
Covered with shells and other jewels of the sea, it had been
made with love by someone with good intentions.

The Warrior was getting closer and closer to the completion of his journey, and instinctively sat near this magical castle of sand.

Then he walked around it several times to admire it's beauty.

He looked at the back of the castle.

He looked at the sides of the castle. He looked at it closely from all angles - from all ways.

And then...

BEHOLD! The Warrior discovered, to his amazement, that
at the entrance of this magnificent castle was a Blue Marble!

The little warrior's heart almost stopped, for this was no ordinary marble, it was a magical marble. This magical blue marble contained the power to transport the warrior into an invisible realm, bursting with love, harmony and total bliss.

The marble was the key that unlocked the invisible door to the land of joy.

This was it! This was what his heart wanted him to discover! This was the purpose of the journey, the reason for his fidgetiness. It was Oh so clear.

"Take the marble!" his heart screamed with delight. "It was placed there by the heavens for you. It is more than a marble, more than a key, more than a symbol. It is a reminder of the precious lessons and experiences you have attained upon following your heart's journey."

For the marble was more than the universe. It was all power, good and evil, working together in peaceful loving harmony. All blended into one mystically magical symphony of love.

The Little Warrior knew that the greatest power in the universe was the power of True Unconditional Love. In knowing this, the Warrior's heart commanded that he gratefully take the magical marble and remember it's many lessons. The Warrior's heart also stated that the Little Warrior should share the marble's magic with other warriors who were as curious and restless as he.

Upon obeying his heart's command, the Little Warrior would attain incredible insights into this symphony of love and the Warrior would be forever protected from the confused and frightened world in which he lived.

The Warrior was a bit confused. He felt it wasn't right to take the marble even though his heart desperately wanted it. The Warrior had mixed feelings. His heart said, "Yes!" His head said, "No!".

So, the Little Warrior decided that, if, tomorrow, he should awake and find that the sand castle with the blue marble at the entrance was still there, perfectly intact, then, in broad daylight when everyone was around to see, he would take the marble.

For then it was truly a gift from the heavens. And a true Warrior can seize a beautiful opportunity in the day. He doesn't have to do it like a thief, in the night.

The Little Warrior excitedly ran home to go to sleep.

The following day the Warrior awakened later than he had anticipated. He dressed hastily, saying to himself,
    "I pray my marble is still there because I know it is truly mine!"

He then ran down to the beach and low and behold, there stood the magical castle with the blue marble at the entrance, untouched and gleaming with brilliance. No one had even seen it! The people were staring right at it, but for some strange reason they could not see it! Even in the daylight!

The Warrior gratefully snatched the marble and held it tightly in the palm of his hand. He faced the scorching sun and thanked the heavens above for the little gift that meant so much to him.

The Little Warrior carried his blue marble everywhere. He even brought it with him under the big tree which shaded him from the hot sun.

But just as the Warrior went to rest under the tree's comfortable shadow, the winds suddenly changed.

A big storm came and, within seconds, washed away the sand castle with all it's precious jewels from the sea.

But, thanks to the restless Warrior, the blue marble and all it's magic was saved.

PUBLISHED by "SIRRI"
P.O. BOX 242
48100 RAVENNA

© COPYRIGHT 1994 PUBLISHED by "SIRRI" di EDGARDO SIRRI

ALL RIGHTS RESERVED. NO PART OF THIS BOOK MAY BE REPRODUCED IN ANY FORM
WITH OUT PERMISSION IN WRITING FROM THE PUBLISHER.
INQUIRIES SHOULD BE ADDRESSED TO:
EDIZIONI SIRRI - CASELLA POSTALE/P.O. BOX 242 48100 - RAVENNA - ITALY

ILLUSTRATIONS by MACRI - GRAFICA by SPADONI

finito di stampare nel 1994
presso GRAFICHE BIESSEZETA S.r.l.
Mazzo do Rho (MI)
Printed in Italy